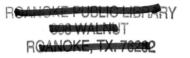
AMBUSH IN THE WILDERNESS

Kris Hemphill

Illustrated by Nicolas Debon

SILVER MOON PRESS
NEW YORK

First Silver Moon Press Edition 2003
Copyright © 2003 by Kris Hemphill
Illustrations copyright © 2003 by Nicolas Debon
Edited by Hope L. Killcoyne

The publisher would like to thank both Doug MacGregor,
Museum Educator at Fort Pitt Museum, and Terry C. Abrams,
President of the Historical Club of the Tonawanda Reservation,
for their historical fact checking.

For information:
Silver Moon Press
New York, NY
(800) 874–3320

Library of Congress Cataloging-in-Publication Data

Hemphill, Kris, 1963-
    Ambush in the Wilderness / Kris Hemphill.
      p. cm.
    Summary: In 1755, after the death of his father, fifteen-year-old Patrick Egan and his
uncle accompany the military force of aide-de-camp George Washington and British
General Braddock as it journeys to fight the French and their Indian allies at Fort
Duquesne in the Ohio River Valley.
    ISBN 1-893110-34-6
    1. United States--History--French and Indian War, 1755-1763--Juvenile fiction. 2.
Washington, George, 1732-1799--Juvenile fiction. [1. United States--History--French and
Indian War, 1755-1763--Fiction. 2. Orphans--Fiction. 3. Ohio River Valley--History--To
1795--Fiction. 4. Washington, George, 1732-1799--Fiction. 5. Frontier and pioneer
life--Ohio River Valley--Fiction.] I. Title.

PZ7.H37745Am 2003
[FIC]--dc21
                                                                    2003045441

10 9 8 7 6 5 4 3 2 1
Printed in the USA

To my parents,
Bob and Shirley Harrison,
with love

–KH

Prologue

The 17th and 18th centuries were a time of tremendous European expansion and aggression. European nations fought for control of lands on their own continent as well as lands abroad. France and England, key combatants, battled each other here in America in four wars spanning nearly seventy-five years. The final and decisive of these wars is known as the *French and Indian War* (1754-1763). *Ambush in the Wilderness* takes place during this war, in the dramatic Battle of the Monongahela. Fought in western Pennsylvania, this two-hour battle was host to the strategic talents and death-defying participation of a twenty-three-year-old volunteer named George Washington.

<u>ONE</u>

Western Pennsylvania
1753

"THERE IT IS, PAPA," CALLED PATRICK. With a gentle squeeze of his heels, Patrick Egan urged his horse into the glade.

He leaned forward in his saddle and eyed the simple log shelter. Except for the roof where a few strips of bark had slipped out of place, everything seemed in order since the last time they had come through on their way to Logstown.

Patrick thought back to when he had helped his father pound the thick stakes into the ground two years earlier. That's when his mother had died, leaving his father no choice but to take Patrick with him on all of his trips to the fur-trading post along the Ohio River. At first, Patrick hated it. He thought the cabin looked as cold and lifeless as he felt. But now at age thirteen, Patrick pretended it was his own private military cabin, like the ones reserved for high-ranking officers in the colonial militia. He smiled.

"'Twill be dark soon," said his father. "We'll take shelter and arrive in Logstown by noon."

John Egan stood tall and fit in his saddle. Born

in Scotland, he was known as a brave, strong, and fair-minded man. Patrick's German mother Anna had said he had "warrior blood" in him. Patrick agreed. Hadn't his father told him, drilled him, that a man's gun and his horse were his most important possessions? Hadn't he talked many times of what it meant to have courage, saying, "Courage is doing what you have to do even when you're scared"?

Patrick watched his father swing down off his mount. He liked the way the horse shifted its weight whenever his father mounted and dismounted. It was as if the horse sensed that the man who held its reins was of great importance. *He is, after all, the finest fur-trader in the Ohio Valley*, thought Patrick.

The October air was still warm and dewy against Patrick's face. It smelled of dry wood chips and moist earth. Wings fluttered softly overhead. Crows cackled. Squirrels scattered. Behind him birch and pine twigs snapped under the hooves of the pack train. There were five horses in all. Each one was tied to the one in front by a rope which now led them into the small meadow. There they'd graze on the sweet grass until satisfied.

The horses snorted and bobbed their heads as Patrick's father loosened their loads. Bulging leather packsaddles sagged under the weight of the merchandise inside: gunpowder, knives, axes, and awls. There were also tomahawks, brass wire, buttons, silver bracelets, and pigs of lead to be melted down for bullets. Patrick pictured the many fine pelts that their goods would buy from their trades with the Indians:

deer, elk, and buffalo and bear skins, along with furs from beaver, wolf, fox, and raccoon.

Patrick hurriedly fastened the leather hobbles on his horse. He hoped it wasn't too late to look for his friend Gwayo.

It had been weeks since he had last seen his Mingo friend. He was a member of the Six Nations Confederacy, what the French called Iroquois, or as they called themselves, Haudenosaunee, the People of the Longhouse. His home was at the mouth of Crow's Run just north of Logstown in a place the white man called Mingo Town.

Patrick scanned the thick, silent woods where his friend liked to hunt. *Where are you, Gwayo?*

"Patrick!"

Patrick turned around. His father was standing in front of the cabin holding a piece of parchment. It was torn at the top where his father had ripped it from the cabin post.

"What is it, Papa?"

"'Tis a note from the French."

Moving closer, Patrick studied his father's face. Dirt and sweat were buried in the creases between his eyes. The muscles in his jaw tightened the way they did whenever his father was deep in thought.

"The king of France is warning all Englishmen to leave the Ohio territory and stay east of the Alleghenies," said his father.

Patrick's face grew hot. He remembered what the friendly Indians had reported earlier that morning: more French soldiers had been spotted paddling down the rivers in their painted canoes. They were noisy as they floated along in their white and blue uniforms chanting the *Te Deum* and shouting, "Vive la France! Vive le Roi!"

And there were French fur traders, too. More of them were encroaching into western Pennsylvania to compete in the purchase of furs.

"The French can't make us leave, can they, Papa? After all, this isn't *their* land."

"Aye," said Patrick's father. "But they claim it is. They care nothing about Sebastian Cabot's voyage giving England her proper claim to the New World. They say they have their own explorers." He stooped down and grabbed a fistful of earth. "News is they're planning to set up a chain of forts along the Ohio and Mississippi Rivers."

French forts—right here along the Ohio River? Patrick could feel his heart pumping in his chest. He slowed his breathing, hoping to appear unshaken by the news. It was the first time his father had talked to him this way—as if he were one of the men at the trading post gathering together to share important information and opinions—and Patrick didn't want him to stop.

Until recently Patrick hadn't worried much about the French or the Indians who sided with them. He knew that some Indians such as the Six Nations remained neutral, choosing not to side with France or England. But there were others—fierce Indians he was told—who could be persuaded. Stories of scalpings and attacks on English colonials surfaced now and again; most, however, occurred farther north and east. Was all that about to change?

Patrick searched for words. "If the French ever caught us, what would they do to us? Take us prisoner?"

His father didn't answer.

"Mr. O'Rourke says they're all talk. Says they're just trying to frighten us." He searched his father's face for a reaction. He could see the muscles in his father's jaw begin to tighten.

"Don't worry, Patrick," said his father. "No Frenchman is going to take us. Not alive, anyway." He ripped the parchment into thin strips and tossed them into a pile of cold ashes. "I'll start the fire," he said.

Patrick tried to take comfort in his father's words. *But what exactly did he mean? Was he serious when he said they wouldn't take them alive?*

Patrick went to work on the cabin floor, hoping to put the matter out of his mind. Carefully he lifted each piece of large bark that blanketed the ground. He was looking for snakes. One morning, having forgotten to check under the bark the night before, Patrick awoke to find a four-foot timber rattlesnake coiled up against his leg. His father grabbed the snake behind the head as calmly as if he had picked up a stick. He sliced the snake into chunks and boiled it over the fire. The juicy meat made a grand breakfast.

As he worked, a strand of black hair fell from Patrick's cap. Briars clung to his leather shirt. His moccasins and leggings, caked with dried mud from fording the creeks, felt like dried cornhusks against his skin. No matter. Patrick liked the way his muddy clothes made him feel as though he were a hard worker like his father.

With no sign of a snake, Patrick began to search the woods for boughs of hemlock to fashion into a soft mattress. Darkness was falling; soon it would be difficult to see.

He had just spotted a branch to harvest when, abruptly, he froze. There was a rustling in the woods. *The shuffle—could it be—human feet?*

Patrick's eyes searched the trees. Nothing. His body was still but his mind was wild—*The French!*

He stiffened. Something moved to his left. *It could be a deer*, he thought. *Or the wind.* Slowly from behind a tree there appeared the unmistakable outline of a man's head. Patrick felt his body turn tingly, weightless.

Before he could react, the thin figure jumped out and began bounding toward him through the trees.

"It's you!" cried Patrick.

Gwayo flashed a broad smile. His name meant "rabbit." Although he had been named by the clan mother at birth—before anyone knew how well the name would suit him—Patrick marveled at how well it did. Gwayo's body, wiry and lithe, moved with such quickness and grace. His face was oval-shaped, thin, with eyes as dark as freshly tilled soil. Patrick had taught him some English and Gwayo, in turn, had helped Patrick to become quite skilled at discovering old Indian footpaths. It was good to see his friend again.

Gwayo held out his hand. Inside was a small rabbit carved out of birch. Often when the two met, they

would exchange small gifts of friendship. Patrick had long understood the importance placed upon such gifts by Gwayo's people.

"It's beautiful," said Patrick, taking the wooden rabbit. He could see from the fine detailing that Gwayo had worked many days on his craft. Of all the trinkets and fancy treasures Patrick had seen at the trading post, he could not recall seeing one as intricate and beautiful as this. "Thank you," he said. "Now I have something for you."

The silver whistle dangled from a leather thong. Smiling, Gwayo took the shiny object and turned it over in his hands to examine it. Then he placed it around his neck.

"Put it in your mouth and blow," instructed Patrick. He demonstrated the action with his own hand and mouth.

Slowly, as if unsure, Gwayo placed the whistle between his lips. With eyes fixed on Patrick, he slowly breathed air into it. Only a soft hiss escaped.

Patrick chuckled. "Blow harder," he said, puffing his cheeks full of air.

Before his friend could respond, Patrick heard a chilling cry.

He spun around toward the cabin. He stood rigid, squinting, waiting for his eyes to adjust to the growing darkness. But horribly, he didn't need his sight to know the source of the familiar call.

It was his father.

And he knew there was but one reaction to that particular sound—the one his father had taught him—*run!*

TWO

PATRICK DIDN'T RUN. HE KNEW HE should, but his legs were as rigid as tree stumps.

Long ago his father had devised the call as a secret signal to warn Patrick when there was great danger at the cabin. "You must listen to me, Patrick," he heard his father say. "If ever you hear that call, you are not to come look or try to help. You are to run until you reach the Walsh's or the MacDermott's."

They had talked about the plan many times. Patrick had discussed it with Gwayo, too, who found it wise and necessary. It seemed perfectly sensible. But somehow hearing the actual call changed all that. Patrick stood transfixed, unable to follow his father's simple instructions. He was standing when he should be running, frozen when he should be reacting.

Before he knew it, Gwayo had pulled Patrick down to a crouching position. On their knees, they crept along the forest floor until they reached a safe position behind a fallen tree. Neither one spoke.

In the fading light, Patrick could see his father. He was standing with his back to the cabin. His gun was leveled at a figure running towards him. He didn't seem aware of the three others creeping up from behind. They were moving fast, closing in around his father.

Now Patrick could see their skin. It was bare and dark. *Indians!*

Someone leaped onto his father's back. A shot rang out. Patrick could see the plume of smoke rise from his father's musket, but no bodies fell.

Patrick reached for his gun. It wasn't there. He suddenly remembered leaning the gun against a stump when he went to collect water from the creek just beyond.

An ache of fear began to gather in the pit of his stomach. *Think! Think!* But what could he do? He had no gun, no horse. Patrick knew Gwayo's tomahawk was useless at this distance. And the whistle? It would only give them away. They were outsized, outarmed, and outnumbered. And everything was happening so quickly!

Patrick turned to his friend. His darkened face was scrunched up, lined with worry.

"Who are they?" Patrick whispered frantically.

Gwayo shook his head. There was, Patrick knew, nothing Gwayo could say. Nothing he could do.

Patrick's eyes darted back to the cabin. His heart sank when he saw the hatchets, three of them, raised high overhead. They came down, swift and silent. Patrick could almost hear the final gasp that

announced death had come. His father's breath, once lusty and clear, drifted into the wilderness, weaving between the pine trees and rising gently over the mountains until it dissipated like smoke in the now chilly night air. Patrick wanted to run after it, but it was gone. Gone forever.

With the pack train in tow, the Indians dashed down the darkened path now as black as a tomb.

It was over.

*　　*　　*

That night Gwayo brought Patrick to his village. After hearing their story, Gwayo's father brought out two of his best horses. "Those who did this to your father are not from our tribe. Go and tell your people. Your father must be buried honorably."

In the morning, Patrick and Gwayo rode to Mr. MacDermott's cabin, just as Patrick's father had instructed him long ago. Mr. MacDermott and another neighbor, Mr. Mullins, traveled back to the shelter with Patrick and Gwayo the following day.

Gwayo helped Patrick choose a burial site behind the cabin next to an old oak tree. The tree stood tall at the edge of the woods. Its thick branches reached out like powerful arms extending over the cabin.

Patrick was grateful that Mr. MacDermott hadn't asked him to take up a shovel; he couldn't bury his own father.

"Bloody savages! They can't be trusted," cried Mr. MacDermott. He scowled at Gwayo. "Not one man in

KRIS HEMPHILL

this land more fair to the Indians than John Egan."

"'Tis true," said Mr. Mullins.

"The French must have put them up to it," said Mr. MacDermott. "Wretched French! First they nail signs to the trees and place lead plates along the river banks with messages proclaiming the country belongs to France. Now this! Slaughtering an honest man like a fresh-killed deer . . ." He shook his head. "I'll tell you this," he said, driving his shovel deep into the earth. "If they think we'll stand by for this, they're wrong. Bloody wrong indeed!"

The men climbed out of the ditch. Patrick knew they were ready to lower his father into the ground. He turned away, staring at Gwayo instead.

Looking at his friend, Patrick felt his heart begin to race as he pictured the dark men with their hatchets sweeping through the air. *Indians. Why would they hurt Papa? He had done nothing to deserve this!* He glared at Gwayo, his head swirling with confusion. *Am I to trust any Indians?* Patrick suddenly dropped his head. *I am a miserable fool. How can I, even for a moment, question Gwayo's loyalty? Am I no better than those Indians whose hearts were full of darkness when they killed Papa? I mustn't—I won't—let my sorrow turn to hatred.*

Patrick looked at the cabin. It showed no signs that he had lost his father—his entire world—just hours before. He could still smell the charred remains of the fire his father had built. The acrid smell seemed to permeate every fiber of Patrick's clothing, every strand of hair. It made him nauseous.

The nausea triggered a rush of despair. Patrick slumped to the ground behind a tree. He pounded the earth with his fist. *How could I forget my gun? What is the matter with me? Why didn't I do something— anything—to help save my father? Do I have no brains at all? No courage?*

Patrick felt a hand on his shoulder. It was Gwayo. "A black cloud has arisen," he said. His face was pale, drawn. "I wipe the tears from your eyes and place your aching heart, which bears you down to one side, in its proper position."

Patrick nodded weakly. He opened his mouth to thank him, but no words came.

"Your father is honorable," said Gwayo. "He is brave like a great warrior chief. His call gave life to me, to you." He paused. "I will repay that life to you."

Patrick tried to understand his meaning. *How could Gwayo ever repay him?*

"Come, lad," called Mr. MacDermott. He was a tall man, lanky, with a scraggly red beard. He was standing with Mr. Mullins next to the mound of freshly turned dirt. In his hand was a Bible.

Patrick made a cross out of sticks and twine, and placed it on the grave. Then he stood alongside Gwayo and the two men in a semi-circle at the foot of the grave. They removed their hats as Mr. MacDermott led them in a short prayer. As he did, Patrick offered up his own silent prayer. But he did not ask for comfort and peace. *Please, God*, he prayed, *don't let them get away with this. If you'd give me but one more chance—just one, I beg—I'll fight them with my last breath!*

"Amen," said Mr. MacDermott. He mopped his brow with the back of his hand. "We best get goin', lad," he said to Patrick, replacing his hat. "'Tis a long way to your Uncle Friedrich's farm."

Patrick didn't want to live with his uncle, Friedrich Bauer. Why couldn't he stay here and live with Gwayo in his longhouse next to the river? He would be a big help to the Indians. He could serve as an interpreter for the tribe and negotiate with the traders to fetch the best price for their furs.

Besides, Patrick knew little of his mother's brother. He had only met him once. Uncle Friedrich's wife, Netta, and twin boys lived with him on their farm in Lancaster, Pennsylvania. The land, Patrick's mother had once said, was rich and green and ran next to the Susquehanna River. She thought it sounded grand. Still, Patrick didn't want to go. The trip would be long; it would take weeks to get there. Worse, he'd never see his friend again.

Patrick tucked the wooden rabbit—now more precious than ever—inside his leather pouch. It was time to say goodbye.

"Gwayo, I don't want to leave you. You're my best friend! When will I ever see you again?"

"We shall meet again, Patrick. You will see." Gwayo hugged Patrick. "Goodbye, my friend."

The old wagon squealed in protest as Patrick climbed in back under the weathered tarp. The smell of wet hay and rotting squash stung his nostrils.

"The Missus sent along this johnnycake," said

Mr. MacDermott. "Made it special for you."

Patrick forced a smile. Although it had been a while since his last meal, his stomach turned when he smelled the food. He buried the cake deep inside his leather pouch.

As the wagon pulled out onto the path, a terrible pain began to rise from within him. It cut through him with razor sharpness. With a steady sureness, the pain grew until he could hold it in no longer. Patrick sobbed, slowly at first and then in great waves. His head throbbed. His eyes burned.

He was all alone with his pain and grief. And there was but one question that haunted his thoughts: What would become of him?

THREE

Lancaster County, Pennsylvania
1755

"PATRICK, ARE YOU OUT THERE?" AUNT Netta stood in the doorway of the stone farmhouse. Her aproned skirt flapped against her swollen belly as the biting January air rushed in. She already had twin boys aged three; Patrick wondered how many little ones she would have this time.

"I'm coming, Aunt Netta." The pierced tin lantern clanked against the stone wall of the barn as Patrick latched the door tight.

When he had first arrived over a year ago and saw the brightly-colored barn, Patrick immediately thought of his mother. The bold red and yellow geometric designs painted on the sides, he knew, were the mark of a Pennsylvania German farm. In Europe these hex signs were believed to keep away evil spirits. "Pure poppycock," his mother had said. "God—not the signs—keeps the evil away."

Patrick marveled at the way in which the barn was built right into the hillside. On cold evenings, Patrick would lay in the hayloft listening to the horses and oxen, all tucked securely away inside the warm earth below, and Patrick would know he was safe, too.

But some nights as he lay in his bed, dark thoughts crept in like a prowler ready to steal whatever hope remained within him. His dreams, when they came, were always the same. Indians would be chasing him, hatchets in hand. Patrick would be running, almost falling, calling out, "Papa! Papa!" But his father never answered. The pounding footsteps of the Indians grew louder and louder until Patrick would feel a hand grip his shoulder.

"Time to get up, Patrick." Patrick, startled and confused, would blink up at Aunt Netta, then sit on the edge of his corn-shuck bed, waiting for his head to clear.

Now, another early winter night descending, the light from his lantern bobbed along the packed earth as he ran to the farmhouse.

When he opened the door, the flames from the fireplace flickered wildly. Shadows danced along the ceiling where dried beans and vegetables hung from the rafters. The room smelled of bacon drippings, sweet cider, and fresh cream. Patrick's empty stomach growled like an angry cat as he walked to the wash basin.

"Any snow yet?" asked Uncle Friedrich. His hands worked the stiff stems of broomcorn, pulling and wrapping them until he could tie them in place on the wooden handle.

"No, sir," answered Patrick. He could feel the heat from the fire now, warming him like a thick woolen blanket.

The twin boys, Jack and Jonas, whined as they tugged at their mama's skirt. Aunt Netta swung the hanging pot from the fire and stirred its contents, ignoring the boys' cries.

Patrick broke off a chunk of hard pretzel and stuffed a small piece into each of the twins' mouths. Their round faces, pink and chapped by the icy wind, brightened.

Uncle Friedrich chuckled. "Patrick, do you know what your mama did when she was that age?"

Patrick shook his head.

"Whenever someone broke off a piece of pretzel, your mama cried because papa told her that the twisted arms of the pretzel were the arms of a worshipper crossed in prayer."

Patrick laughed. It felt good. Laughter had come only sparingly since his father had died.

"Sit, sit," said Aunt Netta.

Patrick took his spot at the end of the bench.

Jack padded over and touched Patrick's leg. "Up, up," he said.

Aunt Netta gave the child a look.

"I don't mind," said Patrick. He lifted the sturdy boy onto his lap. He liked having the boys around, except when they cried. Sometimes just the wind howling through the trees would frighten them to tears. And when one cried, the other followed. Patrick didn't know if the second one was crying because he was scared, too, or if he just felt sad for his twin.

Patrick couldn't remember if the wind had ever made him cry when he was their age. What he could

remember was the smell of his mother's hands when she wiped the tears from his cheeks. They smelled of apple butter. "There, there," she would whisper. "You are a brave boy just like your father, eh?"

Aunt Netta dished out the potato soup and dumplings into wooden bowls called trenchers. "Mustn't forget the sweets and sours," she said. "Can't have a proper meal without seven sweets and seven sours."

She disappeared down the darkened steps leading to the root cellar. Soon she emerged with various crocks, jars, and jugs cradled in her arms. Inside were pickled cabbage, spiced seckel pears, lemon honey, marmalades, green tomato relish, pickled beets, and marinated peppers.

"Heard news about Fort Duquesne," said Uncle Friedrich.

Aunt Netta looked up. "Oh?"

"The British have sent troops. They've come to take back the fort from the French."

Just eighteen miles from Logstown, Fort Duquesne was located at the forks of the Ohio where the Monongahela and Allegheny Rivers joined to form the Ohio River. It was a strategic site. Whoever occupied it would have control over the rivers, which meant control over the fur trade in the Ohio Valley. Last spring, Governor Dinwiddie had sent Virginia troops to the Forks to build a British fort called Fort Prince George. Soon thereafter, however, French forces attacked and took over the fort. The French built their own fort, naming it Fort Duquesne. It seemed to Patrick that colonial fur traders like his father would never again be able to trade in the Ohio Valley. The only encouraging news, however, came last May when a lieutenant colonel of the Virginia militia led an attack on a French scouting party not far from the fort. Ten Frenchmen were killed, including their commander, Jumonville. Still, Patrick understood that unless the British re-captured the fort, the French would retain control over the region.

"Seems they've sent two British regiments from Ireland to lead in the fight," said Uncle Friedrich. "I suppose they think the British army knows more about fightin' than our own."

Aunt Netta stood up and walked slowly to the fireplace. She stirred the kettle but said nothing.

Uncle Friedrich took notice. His face softened as he spoke. "Netta, you mustn't fret. There's nothing to worry about. We haven't declared war."

She looked at Uncle Friedrich and nodded. Patrick, too, wanted to ease her worry, to assure her that everything would be alright. But he knew not to trust such sayings. His own father had said as much just before he died.

Jonas jumped up and down. "Schnitz, schnitz!" he shouted.

"Yes, Jonas," said Aunt Netta, absently. "You'll have your apple schnitz pie."

Patrick and Uncle Friedrich turned their empty trenchers upside down. Aunt Netta placed a thick slab of the dried fruit pie onto the pie side of their bowls.

"I'm not being asked to go," said Uncle Friedrich.

"No," agreed Netta. "I suppose not."

*   *   *

By late April, everyone in Lancaster was talking about the plans to take over Fort Duquesne. Patrick learned that British General Edward Braddock would be leading the expedition. At age sixty, he had forty-five years of army service, but he had never before fought in the wilderness.

Patrick came in with the milking pail. Muddy brown clumps dripped from his boots onto Netta's clean floor. He quickly sat down and removed them.

"I don't like the sound of it," he heard his aunt say.

Patrick peered around the corner. Aunt Netta was sitting at her loom weaving her linen and wool yarn together to make linsey-woolsey cloth. She was talking to Uncle Friedrich. Beside her was the cradle where baby Katie slept. "We're Quakers. We're not fighting people."

"Netta, we may not have a choice," said Uncle Friedrich. He was holding a newspaper, the *Pennsylvania Gazette.* "General Braddock is still in great need of wagons, horses, and men to carry out his expedition. It says here he'll pay us 15 shillings per day for our wagon and four horses. Besides, if I don't hire them out now, the General may have them dragooned into the army."

"But the wagon and horses are our livelihood," said Aunt Netta. She fingered her yarn nervously. "And how can we be sure they won't work our horses to death?"

Uncle Friedrich looked out the small window to

his right. Rain tapped loudly against the sill like the distant roll of drums. "I'll have to go," he said in a low voice. "I'll drive my own team and wagon. It's the only way."

"Oh, Friedrich." Aunt Netta picked up the baby and held her tight against her chest.

Almost without thinking, Patrick stepped into the room. "Take me with you, Uncle Friedrich. I can handle a gun. Papa taught me."

"We're not being asked to be soldiers," said Uncle Friedrich. "Just carry provisions. That's all."

"Yes sir."

Uncle Friedrich considered. "Just the same, I suppose we need to be prepared to defend ourselves." He was silent for a moment. Then he shook his head. "I don't know. You're needed here, too."

Patrick looked at Aunt Netta. She looked so fragile holding Katie behind the big wooden loom. "Your papa, bless his soul—I suppose he would have taken you had he been asked." Her eyes were wet with tears. She straightened and with quick hands began patting the round bundle in her arms. "I've got able neighbors. And there's Doctor Hofstetter if I have a need."

Patrick locked eyes with Uncle Friedrich.

"I suppose an extra pair of hands wouldn't hurt," said his uncle. Turning to Aunt Netta he said, "I'll send for your brother and Leah to stay with you."

Aunt Netta nodded.

"I can go then?" asked Patrick.

There was a long pause. "All right then," said Uncle Friedrich. "We leave next week."

FOUR

"YEE!" AT THE SOUND OF UNCLE Friedrich's voice, Patrick awoke. Immediately he felt the wagon turn left at the command. The great wheels of the Conestoga creaked as they bumped onto a road deeply pitted with ruts and grooves left by an assortment of wagons pulled by oxen and horses.

Patrick sat up and rubbed his eyes. A stiff breeze rustled the tender leaves of the white oaks and tulip poplars that stretched along the road like soldiers standing guard. Ruby-crowned kinglets perched high on the branches singing out, "look-at-me, look-at-me, look-at-me!" Their song's subtle trilling rattled Patrick's sense of calm on that unexpectedly chilly May morning.

Two weeks had passed since they had left Lancaster. With each day, Patrick grew increasingly anxious. He had convinced Uncle Friedrich to take him along on the expedition. Now he wondered if he should have come at all. Back on the farm he had felt so courageous, jumping at the chance to face the enemy who killed his father. But as he inched closer to their destination, Patrick began to question everything. *What if Mr. MacDermott is wrong? What if the French didn't send the Indians to kill Papa? The Indians could have acted alone. Either way, the French are trying to claim the very land Papa and I called home. If Papa were alive, he'd come to fight the French.* But one question continued to haunt Patrick: if he were to encounter the enemy, would he stand by and do nothing, just as he had when his father died, or would he fight like his father?

Above the steady drone of horses' hooves striking the packed dirt, Patrick heard voices in the distance. Somewhere behind them a horse whinnied. Peering out the back, Patrick saw two wagons coming up the road. Trailing them were a few pack horses and several men on foot.

It can't be much farther, thought Patrick.

Fort Cumberland, where Wills Creek slips into the Potomac River, was the official starting place for the expedition. Patrick knew that many, including General Braddock himself, would be arriving from Braddock's headquarters in Alexandria, Virginia. He wondered if the men following behind had come to join the campaign.

The sun had dipped behind the mountains when the wagon rolled into a stretch of rocky land at the foot of Wills Mountain. In the distance, Patrick spotted a long fence of stout wooden stakes rising up from the ground. Just beyond was Wills Creek; to the south, the Potomac River. "We made it!" he cried.

Rising above the line of pickets, Patrick could

see the star-shaped log stockade called Fort Cumberland. Having once been a small trading post, the fort had been enlarged to support the supplies and troops necessary for the army's advance on Fort Duquesne. *How Papa would have loved to have traded here!*

As they made their way across the open field, Patrick could see men young and old, hundreds of them. He had never before seen so many people in one place. Some were hauling water buckets down a long trench that led to the creek, while others streamed in and out of the fort's front gate carrying large bags across their backs. New arrivals went to work setting up tents and unloading their packs. Horses grazed on the tender spring shoots of grass, which had been turned brown by the recent drought.

As Uncle Friedrich pulled the wagon up near the fort's gate, Patrick noticed two groups of soldiers gathered in the clearing next to the fort. With them appeared to be two officers on horseback. "What are they doing?" asked Patrick.

"Drilling," answered Uncle Friedrich. "The soldiers must practice if they are to be ready to attack the French." He dismounted. "Unhitch the horses while I report our arrival."

While Patrick loosened the harnesses, he couldn't stop watching the soldiers drill. The British soldiers, known as regulars, were clad in scarlet coats and brown marching gaiters that extended above the knee. Upon their heads were tall, pointed caps. Their five-foot musket, known as "The Brown Bess," could hit a man up to 80 yards away.

The colonial troops, provincials as they were called, dressed more simply. Some wore everyday clothes while others donned smart blue militia coats or green hunting shirts and leggings. They may have looked scruffier than the British, but their flintlock rifles, similar to Patrick's, could hit a target 300 yards away.

"They're a miserable lot," said a British soldier standing nearby. He and a fellow comrade were watching the provincials form their lines. "Every colonist should kiss our boots for coming here to save their hides. All His Majesty asks is that they provide supplies and a few good soldiers, and look at them! Spiritless. Unsoldierlike. Some look as though they've just escaped from prison. And the food. . . It's not fit for a dog! An entire wagonload of salt beef had to be buried this morning because it arrived spoiled—no pickle in the casks!"

His comrade shook his head in disgust. "It's the wagoner's fault. He probably drained the pickle to lighten his load. We'll no doubt die of the bloody flux before we ever reach Fort Duquesne."

"Move aside!" came a booming voice.

Patrick turned to see a team of seven large horses thundering toward him. He jumped sideways, almost stumbling, as the horses' hooves came within inches of his feet. Hitched to the team was a carriage-mounted field gun, a "six-pounder" in British military terms. The bronze cannon was monstrous as it rolled past, stirring great clouds of dust.

"That's nothin'," said a boy standing next to Patrick, who seemed to have appeared out of the dust. He looked several years older than Patrick, a foot taller perhaps, with stringy blond hair. He wore leather breeches and a simple shirt that had most likely been white at one time. He was holding a flintlock rifle. "They got bigger guns—'ship killers'—firing twelve-pound balls that could sink a ship in one blast," he said. "They belong to the *H.M.S. Norwich*. Problem is, there ain't no good way to get 'em over the mountains."

Patrick was silent, not certain that the boy was speaking to him.

"Gotta name?" asked the boy, turning towards him.

"Patrick Egan."

"I'm Will. Will Jenkins." He stepped back and eyed Patrick from head to toe. "You come to fight?"

Patrick, uncomfortable in the boy's beady, taunting gaze, wanted to lie. He didn't like the way the boy was questioning him as if he had no business being here. "I've come with my uncle. We've been asked to carry ammunition."

The boy turned and spat on the ground. He brought his flintlock rifle up to his eye and aimed it at a tree. "I can shoot the eye of a squirrel at fifty paces. I drill regular." Will lowered his gun and eyed Patrick. "Got a gun?"

"I do," said Patrick, straightening. He wished he hadn't left it in the wagon.

Will sneered. "Better know how to use it."

*　　*　　*

By evening, more provincials had filed into camp. Most were from Virginia. The rest came from Maryland, New York, and South Carolina. They were organized into companies called Rangers.

One member of the Virginia Rangers was a tall, broad-shouldered man named Fritz. His blue militia coat was frayed at the cuffs and his leggings were worn through on his right knee. He talked in a loud voice and didn't seem to mind if he had a willing audience or not.

"I tell yeh," said Fritz, "these British don't know the first thing about fightin' in the wilderness. They come here in their fancy red coats and think they can fight like they do in Europe, all proper in their straight lines facing their enemy like gentlemen about to have tea. I know. I fought at Fort Necessity a year ago under Colonel Washington." He bit off a chunk of smoked meat. "We're lucky we survived," he said, shaking his head. "The Indians—they fight like wild beasts, not honorable like the redcoats are expecting. If they surprise us in the woods, we're as good as dead!"

Two British soldiers walking past suddenly stopped. They fixed their eyes on Fritz.

"They're savages. Crueler than demons!" cried Fritz. His eyes shifted briefly to the British soldiers standing nearby. His loud voice seemed to grow even louder as the British soldiers looked on. "The poor soul who wanders from camp or lags behind—he's fair game to their savage ways. Scalpings, torture, cannibalism. . . Nothing is beyond 'em."

Patrick closed his eyes and shuddered. "Savages" was how Mr. MacDermott had described the Indians who massacred his father. Hearing it again, Patrick felt the corn chowder in his stomach churn like butter.

"The French have hundreds of Indians on their side," said Fritz. He waved a finger in the direction of the woods beyond. "They're out there. Probably watching us right now."

The British soldiers craned their necks toward the trees, squinting.

Watching them, Fritz became more animated as he spoke. "They care nothin' for the gentlemanly ways of Braddock's men. They hide behind trees and sneak up on yeh before yeh can rip open the cartridge paper with yer teeth."

There was a nervous silence.

"Not all Indians love the French," said Uncle Friedrich. "A group from the Susquehanna is here at camp; some have brought their wives and children. And there's talk of Cherokee and Catawba joining us."

Fritz laughed. "Are yeh daft? Indians are not to be trusted. They change their allegiance more often than the wind shifts direction! Besides, Braddock is too proud to accept help from the Indians. As for the women and children—he won't stand for it in his camp. They'll be gone by mornin'."

Fritz was right. The next day, Braddock ordered all the Indian women to leave camp. When they did, their Indian men went with them. Only eight returned the following day.

At sundown, as Patrick helped Uncle Friedrich build a fire, the Indians' sudden departure from camp weighed heavily on his mind. There was so much he didn't understand. *Why wouldn't the General welcome anyone willing to help us fight, Indian or not?*

Uncle Friedrich stretched out on his back next to the fire and closed his eyes. Patrick, unable to rest, sat hunched over on the other side, staring into the flames. A low buzz of chatter filled the camp as men talked and shared humorous stories before bedding down for the night. Patrick wanted desperately to talk about what had happened between the Indians and General Braddock, but he knew not to disturb Uncle Friedrich. He waited. After a time, he saw his uncle's hand swipe at something crawling on his neck. Patrick spoke up. "Why did the Indian men leave?"

Uncle Friedrich turned and looked at Patrick. Slowly he stood up and stirred the fire with the pointed end of a stick. Sparks snapped and flew into the air. Patrick watched them die out as they fell to the ground.

"Their people were insulted," said Uncle Friedrich. "Fritz says chiefs from the Delaware, Shingas, and Mingo nations met with General Braddock. They asked him if the Indians friendly to the English would be permitted to live and trade among us and have sufficient hunting ground to support their families. Braddock refused. He said, 'No savage will inherit the land.' So they left."

A Mingo chief was here? Patrick thought of Gwayo and his father. For a moment he felt ashamed. How could he consider supporting General Braddock, a man who refused to show honor to Gwayo's people?

"Does the General not trust *any* Indians?" asked Patrick.

"Perhaps," said Uncle Friedrich, studying the fire. "Like Fritz said, plenty of Indian tribes have switched their allegiance to the French. I'm sure the General knows what he's doing."

Patrick hoped he was right.

FIVE

"GUNPOWDER AND CASE SHOTS, I SEE," said a stocky man peering into the back of the wagon. He was the wagon master in charge of forty wagons, including Uncle Friedrich's.

The wagon master climbed up under the wagon's white homespun cover where Patrick had stacked the ammunition. Carefully, he began counting the case shots. These cloth bags held small, round iron pellets which, when fired from a cannon with gunpowder, were a deadly shot at close range.

"Everything appears in order," said the man, marking his ledger. Without looking up he asked, "You from Pennsylvania?"

"Yes. Lancaster," answered Uncle Friedrich.

The wagon master nodded. "If it weren't for the good work of Mr. Benjamin Franklin, the General would be cursing your kind in Pennsylvania like he has the other colonies. He's been fussing over the shortage of wagons ever since he got here, saying the colonies promised everything but delivered nothing. Thanks to Pennsylvania, there are now enough wagons

and pack horses to haul the army's food and supplies."
The wagon master made another mark in his ledger.
"You are to report to me every day. General's orders."
His eyes fell on Patrick's rifle. "Remember, no drivers
are called to do the duty of a soldier. Still, one should
be prepared. After all, this *is* war."

For a moment, no one spoke. Patrick looked at
Uncle Friedrich. Noticing his glance, Uncle
Friedrich shifted his feet and quickly looked away.
Expedition, not war, was how Uncle Friedrich had
described their journey. But as Patrick considered
the wagon master's words, he realized that perhaps
he had not fully considered all that might be
involved in an advance toward Fort Duquesne.
Watching his uncle, the thought occurred to Patrick:
perhaps Uncle Friedrich hadn't either.

*   *   *

JUNE 9, 1755

The air was muggy and still when Patrick awoke.
In the pre-dawn darkness he heard the shouts of
officers rousing their men from sleep. *Today we
begin our 112-mile march to Fort Duquesne*, Patrick
told himself. He pulled the quilt closer around him,
catching a smell of clean linen. The sweet, crisp
scent reminded him of Aunt Netta and the twins.
How far away it all seemed to him now.

Just as Patrick was realizing that he hadn't had
the nightmare of the Indians chasing him that night,

Fritz's loud, cranky voice broke into his thoughts.

"We're six weeks behind schedule," grumbled Fritz. "Each day we delay is another day the French have to gather more soldiers, more guns, and—worse—more savages!"

"Pipe down, Fritz!" said a British soldier.

"Just telling yeh like it is," he answered. "I don't care for the way we're getting started, that's all. Gives me a bad feeling."

"Well, I don't care for your incessant jabbering about the savages," said the soldier. "Not one of their lot shall come against the King's regulars with any success."

Patrick crawled out of his bedding, picturing the Frenchmen chanting in their painted canoes, laughing all the way to the fort. He tried to relax, to trust in the strength of the 2,000 men gathered about him. They were, after all, expertly trained soldiers, heavily armed, and led by a highly experienced General. These men would eat, sleep, and travel with him for the next several weeks. *I would be well served to trust them,* he told himself. He sat next to his folded bedding and closed his eyes. There was nothing to do now but sit and wait for the wagon train to be called.

The morning seemed endless. Hours passed before the advance guard assembled and pulled out of camp. Leading the way was a small number of guides, three hundred soldiers under Lieutenant Colonel Thomas Gage, and a party of axmen and laborers. Their task was to clear a road twelve-feet wide through the rugged, dense forest so that the troops, wagons, and artillery could follow.

It was early afternoon before Patrick's wagon was called.

"Ready?" called Uncle Friedrich.

"Yes, sir," answered Patrick.

The team lurched forward. Patrick watched from the back of the wagon as the great train of ammunition and artillery wagons followed behind like a long, loosely-jointed snake. There were also soldiers, pack horses, oxen, and cattle. Thirty sailors were on hand to assist in dragging the artillery over the mountains. Several of the soldiers' wives joined the march— washerwomen they were called—as well as a number of hired nurses to tend to the sick.

Slowly the wagon curved its way around Wills Mountain. Uncle Friedrich whistled as they moved along the newly hewed road, which before had been little more than an old Indian footpath. The ride was rough; thick tree roots and knobby underbrush littered their path.

A collage of trees and thick vegetation began to appear as they headed west along the new road. Black locust trees, chestnuts, and vine-draped white pines provided cool shade from the hot June sun. Blue violets dotted the shady groves on either side of the path, filling the air with a hint of sweetness. But no matter where they went, a fine film of dirt seemed to cover everything. Patrick could taste it. He could feel it in his hair, on his clothes, under his nails, and between his teeth.

"Whoa!" called Uncle Friedrich.

The wagon came to a sudden stop. Patrick jumped out to look. Just ahead was a steep ridge on the eastern slope of Savage Mountain.

"Stand back," called Uncle Friedrich. Sitting atop the wheel horse, he gave a tug on the jerk line. The line tightened against a set of small brass rings. They jingled, signaling the horses to pull forward. "Nice and easy, now," he said. Slowly, the wagon eased safely over the ridge.

The grade, however, was too great for the wagon behind them; two of its wheels shattered when it hit a boulder.

"At this pace," said Uncle Friedrich, "we'll be lucky if we get to Fort Duquesne before the rivers ice over."

Patrick marched beside the wagon, stopping only to claw at the chiggers and wood ticks that burrowed under his skin. The air was thick with flies and mosquitoes. Gnats, swarms of them, flew into his nose and mouth. Dirt stung his eyes. His shirt clung to his back, wet with perspiration, and for once Patrick was thankful he wasn't one of the men wearing a militia coat.

They had only advanced two hundred yards when they stopped again.

"Now what?" called a teamster behind them.

"Patience, men," chided an officer on horseback. "With so many streams and gorges, bridges must be built to accommodate the column."

"Column?" said the teamster sarcastically. "We're more like a four-mile bloody slug!"

* * *

June 18, 1755

No one spoke as they passed through an eerie, dark patch of woods known as the Shades of Death. The tops of the towering white pines intertwined overhead, creating a deep gloom that sent a shiver down Patrick's spine. He knew that such a darkened place could hide an enemy all too well.

They followed the road past Red Ridge and into a valley called the Little Meadows where they camped for the night.

"I thought we'd be farther along," said Patrick. "We've been traveling for over a week and Fritz says we've not gone but three miles each day."

"We'll move along faster once they split the column," said Uncle Friedrich. "General Braddock wants to press forward with a lighter force. Tomorrow we'll forge ahead with the bulk of the army. The rest will stay back with Colonel Dunbar and follow at their own pace."

The next day, Patrick and Uncle Friedrich left before dawn with the rest of the streamlined force. It was mid-morning the following day when the wagon master ordered Uncle Friedrich to stop.

"One of the General's close aides has become ill," said the wagon master. "The services of your wagon are needed to carry him until such time as he is fit to rejoin the march. Until then, the General has ordered that you drop back with Colonel Dunbar's detachment."

Drop back with Colonel Dunbar? thought Patrick. *We'll never make it to Fort Duquesne!*

Moments later, two British captains placed a man in the back of Uncle Friedrich's wagon. Patrick could see that the man, in his early twenties perhaps, was dressed as an officer with the Virginia Militia. With his body stretching a full foot beyond the five foot musket that lay beside him, the man appeared to be among the tallest at camp. He was solidly built, with hands as big and powerful as any Patrick had ever seen. His cheeks, though, were flushed, his eyes bloodshot. Under the thick woolen blanket, his great body shook with fever.

Patrick turned and whispered to Uncle Friedrich, "Who is he?"

"His name is George Washington," whispered Uncle Friedrich. "One of the General's aides-de-camp."

The sick man strained to lift his head. "I have a request for the General," he said shakily.

"What is your pleasure?" asked the captain.

"Ask the General if he would send for me before he reaches Fort Duquesne."

"I shall ask him and report back to you," said the captain. "You, son," he said, pointing to Patrick, "are to tend to his horse and bring him food and drink as necessary. If he worsens, send for the nurse immediately."

Patrick went to work fetching fresh water from the creek. Washington slept most the day, awakening only briefly to sip the cool water. Despite the June heat, Washington kept his leather shoes on and pulled the heavy blanket up close to his chin.

The next day, a messenger arrived with a note for Washington. He gave it to Patrick with instructions to deliver it when the colonel awakened.

By late afternoon, Washington was awake and requesting water.

"Sir," said Patrick, handing him a flask of water. "A note arrived for you from General Braddock."

Washington pulled himself up to a sitting position. His face was pale and his eyes swollen. "Can you read, lad?" he asked Patrick.

"Yes, sir."

Washington closed his eyes and motioned with his hand for Patrick to begin.

Nervously, Patrick slid his finger under the paper, breaking the crimson wax seal. Unfolding the letter, he read:

I give my word of honor that I will call you to the front before we reach the fort, provided the surgeon is in agreement. In the meantime, I recommend Doctor James's powders to speed your recovery. Honorably, General Braddock.

Washington, his eyes still closed, nodded slowly and fell back to sleep. He didn't move until the surgeon arrived the next morning with Colonel Dunbar's detachment. Patrick watched as the surgeon administered a powdery medicine to Washington. "Bring him plenty of water," he told Patrick, "lest he become dehydrated."

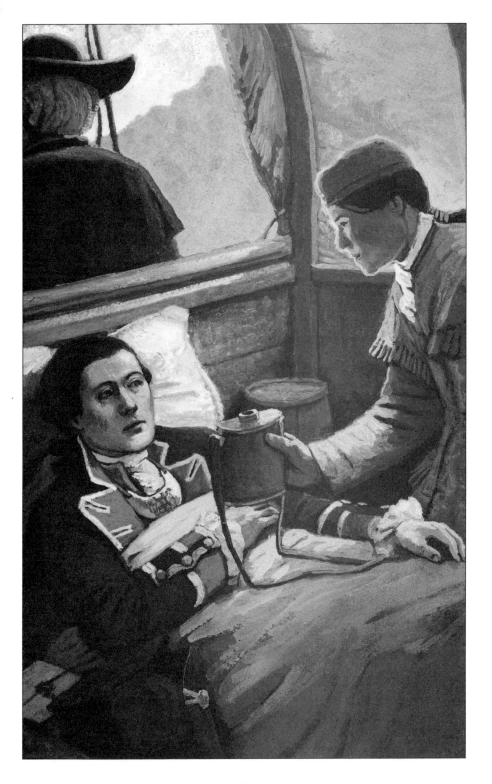

*   *   *

JUNE 22, 1755

Early in the morning, Patrick overheard Washington talking to the surgeon.

". . . the most excellent medicine," said Washington. "I feel immediate relief. Surely you will release me to return to duty."

"You are still with fever," said the surgeon. "You may continue in the wagon with Colonel Dunbar's division, but you are not yet well enough to rejoin General Braddock. Doing so would put your life at risk."

Washington closed his eyes, clearly pained by the doctor's report. After the surgeon left, he called for Uncle Friedrich. "Have we any news from the front?"

"I hear three of our soldiers who had slipped past the sentinels were shot a few days ago by Indian allies of the French," said Uncle Friedrich. "The General is offering a reward for every scalp of an enemy Indian taken by one of our soldiers."

Washington shook his head. "We can't afford to lose any more Indian scouts." Turning to Patrick he asked, "What do you think?"

The question stunned Patrick. "I . . . I agree, sir."

Washington smiled. "What is your name, lad, and where are you from?"

"Patrick Egan, sir." Patrick considered Washington. Though he was no more than ten years older than Patrick, there was a seriousness, an air of great importance about him that quietly demanded respect. Indeed, his very size spoke of solidity and power. Washington's role as a colonel a year earlier only added to his aura. Patrick told him about living with Uncle Friedrich and Aunt Netta on their farm in Lancaster.

"What became of your own parents?" Washington asked.

"My mother died four years ago. The fever took her," said Patrick, sadly.

"And your father?"

Patrick shifted uncomfortably. He had not spoken of his father since his death.

Patrick cleared his throat. "He was killed, sir. Indians. Hostile Indians."

Washington remained silent for several minutes. Patrick wondered if he was waiting to hear more about his father's death. Then, to Patrick's amazement, Washington said, "I, too, lost my father when I was about your age." He gave a look that seemed to say that he understood, that everything would be all right.

"Patrick," said Washington, smiling, "you remind me a little of myself when I was younger. You see, I nursed my half-brother Lawrence when he was sick. He suffered with terrible fevers and headaches, much like I have now."

"What happened to him?" asked Patrick.

"I'm afraid he died."

Patrick looked down, wishing he hadn't asked the question. He wondered if Washington feared he, too, would die from his illness.

Washington sat up, straightening his coat. "I trust that Providence has not placed me here in vain. I *shall* recover. And when I do, I will endeavor to fulfill the purpose for which I have come to serve in this campaign. Since the day my men and I fired on a French scouting party last May, I have known that armed conflict with the French would be inevitable."

"It was you, sir, who led the assault that killed the ten Frenchmen?" Patrick asked with great interest.

Washington paused. Then he said, "It was I. And I am certain that we've much to overcome if we are to be victorious over the French. I fear a great many Indians have come to their aid. Their style of wilderness fighting could prove formidable against our slow advancing army."

Patrick sat silent, considering Washington's words.

"Is there something you want to ask me, lad?"

Patrick hesitated. "Have you ever . . . do you ever fear for your safety?"

Washington smiled. "God defended me from all harm at Fort Necessity, and before as I set out on a perilous journey to Fort LeBoeuf. I trust he will do so now. And you?"

Patrick didn't answer.

SIX

July 8, 1755

AFTER SEVERAL WEEKS OF ILLNESS, Washington was pronounced healthy enough to return to the main division. Still somewhat weak and dizzy, Washington lay in Uncle Friedrich's wagon as it trudged toward Braddock's camp. Patrick followed behind on Washington's long-legged chestnut horse.

When they arrived at Braddock's camp Patrick was surprised to find the troops in high spirits. As the soldiers pitched their tents on the east bank of the Monongahela River, just twelve miles from Fort Duquesne, most agreed that by the following evening the King's Colours would be flying high above the parapet of the French fort.

"That is, if the French don't blow up their fort before we get there," said a familiar voice. It was Will Jenkins. He stretched out on the ground next to Patrick and stared up at the sky. Patrick continued inspecting his rifle, pretending not to notice.

Will sighed. "If the French only knew we were but a day's march away, they'd blow up their stores and—"

"What makes you think they aren't watching us?

They've got Indian scouts," Patrick reminded him.

Will chuckled. "A few, perhaps. *You* seen any?"

Patrick pulled back the hammer and felt the piece of flint for sharpness. "No, but I know they're out there," he answered. "We'd be wise to have more Indians on our side."

"Too late for that," said Will. "A group of Ohio Indians just left."

Patrick bristled. *How could Braddock have let another band of Indians just go away?*

"They offered to help us fight—something about wanting to preserve Indian land for the Indians . . ." Will yawned and closed his eyes. "Anyway, the General sent them away. He said he didn't come all this way to let a bunch of savages take over His Majesty's victory."

Friendly Indians—rejected again! If the Indians had been angry and insulted the first time, they were bound to be downright furious by now. *I must get word to Colonel Washington,* thought Patrick, rising to his feet. *If we don't get the Indians back, they'll head to one of two places: home, or to join the French!*

Patrick ran through the camp. *This is our last chance to convince the General that*—Patrick stopped. He was stunned to find Washington on his feet. He was entering General Braddock's tent. Although his face was ashen, he stood tall and spoke with a clear, strong voice.

Patrick inched closer to the tent and listened.

"Sir," he heard Washington say, "I believe we could make good use of our Indian friends as scouts. They know how to fight in the wilderness; they would be more apt to uncover enemy Indians waiting to ambush—"

"Those enemy savages," came Braddock's voice, booming through the tent, "may frighten continental troops, but they can make no impression on the King's regulars!"

* * *

JULY 9, 1755

"Hurry along, men!" barked a corporal.

In the dim morning light, Patrick watched as men scrambled about in various stages of dress. Teamsters hitched their horses, officers inspected the artillery, and soldiers became fully accoutered.

Patrick ate a dry, hard biscuit. He tried to pretend it was a piece of Netta's warm apple schnitz. *It won't be long now*, thought Patrick.

He quickly saddled and harnessed Washington's horse.

Washington winced as he lifted his foot to the stirrup. His breathing became heavy and his legs trembled. Patrick wondered how anyone in his condition could endure the jolting of a fast-moving horse.

"Wait, sir!" called Patrick. He grabbed a pillow and strapped it to Washington's saddle using a strip of leather he salvaged from his cartridge box.

Washington chuckled. "You're a fine lad, Patrick Egan."

Suddenly the drums of the Forty-fourth erupted

like a clap of thunder. Drums and fifes played the Grenadier's March as the advance party, in double ranks, began to file out of camp.

Washington mounted his horse. With a nod and a tip of his hat, he rode off to join Braddock and his staff.

"Aren't you supposed to be back with the other wagoners?"

Patrick turned around. It was Will.

"My company is supposed to march alongside your wagon train as guards," said Will. "Even the General can see you need protection."

"I can hold my own," said Patrick testily.

Will chuckled. "Ever see an Indian kill a man?"

Patrick glared at Will. The recollection of his father's death seared through his memory like a white hot arrow. The muscles in his hand slowly tightened into a fist.

"Well, *I* have," said Will. "That's why I drill. I can prime, load, and fire three times a minute. Not one Indian is gonna slip past me. You ought to be thankful that the General has posted me to protect you."

Patrick clenched his fist tighter until his knuckles turned bone white. Turning, he planted his legs firmly in the ground facing Will. Like a coiled snake ready to strike, Patrick drew back his fist. Just as he was about to unleash his fury, Patrick heard Uncle Friedrich call out behind him.

"Patrick, we've orders to fall in behind Colonel Gage's advance guard and proceed toward the Monongahela River."

Hearing Uncle Friedrich approach, Patrick lowered his fist but kept his eyes trained on Will. Will attempted to return the look but suddenly turned and walked away.

"The terrain along the river's east bank is said to be too rough to pass," continued Uncle Friedrich, "so we'll cross to the river's west bank near the mouth of Crooked Run. From there we'll go on until we reach Turtle Creek, where we'll cross back over to the east bank. That will put us on track for our final approach to the . . ."

If I ever get the chance, thought Patrick, *I'll show him I'm not afraid to—*

"Did you hear me?" snapped Uncle Friedrich.

"Yes, sir."

Up ahead, Patrick could see General Braddock readying the main troops, arranging them in straight columns. Will was lining up along the flank, just one wagon length away.

"Make final preparations!" called a voice to the teamsters. "We shall move out with the main troops once Colonel Gage has cleared the way."

Another hour passed before Patrick and the rest of the ammunition wagons and artillery pulled out of camp. Cannons, howitzers, and mortars filled the road. Patrick wondered what it would feel like to fire a twelve-pound ball from a cannon. Fritz claimed the larger cannons could fire a shot 900 yards, more than three times the distance of his own flintlock rifle.

The sun was high in the sky when Patrick and Uncle Friedrich reached the top of the Monongahela's embankment. The rushing water sounded like a thousand hissing snakes. As they waited for orders to proceed, tiny droplets of sweat began to gather on Patrick's forehead.

Down below, Braddock's men crossed the river without incident. The recent drought had left the water shallow, barely reaching the soldiers' knees. Patrick thought the men looked splendid in full uniform, the sun glistening brilliantly off their brass helmets and bayonets. But as Patrick watched the soldiers scramble up the far bank, he wondered how the wagons would fare scaling the muddy ridge.

"Move out!" came a voice.

Uncle Friedrich gave a quick tug on the jerk line. At once, the horses eased down the bank toward the water's edge. With drums beating in the distance, the horses plunged into the water. The wagon's huge wheels sliced through the cool water as the horses picked their way over the slippery rocks along the riverbed. The wagon bumped along, rumbling and creaking.

Midway across the river, with 100 yards to go, Patrick had a terrible thought. *If the enemy is planning an ambush, this would be the place to do it.*

Patrick pulled his rifle close to his chest. Nervously, he brought his cartridge box and powder horn around in front of him. He opened the cartridge box with one hand. He waited.

There was no sign of the enemy.

Once across, the horses strained to pull up the muddy bank. The wet, sloppy ground grabbed at the wheels, pulling and sucking, until the wagon came to a stop. Patrick jumped out. They were halfway up the bank. With every turn of the wheel, the wagon seemed to sink deeper into the soggy earth.

Uncle Friedrich cracked his whip high in the air.

The wagon surged forward and then rolled back. It rocked back and forth until, finally, it pulled free from the mud.

When they reached dry ground, Patrick let out a sigh of relief. So far, everything was proceeding as planned. Still, he felt uneasy. He didn't like being sandwiched between forest and river with no easy escape route. The woods could be full of enemy Indians. *But why hadn't they shown themselves?* Maybe Will was right. Maybe the French had left the fort long ago.

It was early afternoon when they reached the second ford. Patrick was relieved to find the bank less steep than the first. The afternoon sun had helped to keep the ground dry and the footing firm. The team splashed through the river and climbed up the far bank with ease.

Once across, soldiers laughed and hugged each other. "We bloody made it!" one man cried. "Long live the King!"

The wagon master was smiling, too, when he rode up to Uncle Friedrich. "The advance guard is clearing our final passage to the fort," he announced. "Graze your horses if you wish while we await further orders."

The woods along the east bank were thick with hemlocks and tall pines, but not as thick as they were in the mountains. The axmen up ahead continued to fell trees and hack away at the thickets to clear a twelve-foot road.

Patrick unhooked the harness buckles and led the horses over a felled tree, into a clearing where the grass was high and plentiful. His cartridge box and powder horn slapped against his thigh as he stepped through the tall grass.

Patrick rested the butt of his rifle on the grass and rubbed his sore shoulder muscles. As the horses devoured the lush grass, Patrick noticed a towering oak nearby. Moving closer, he saw that a ring of bark had been stripped away. On the exposed surface were threatening pictures of dead men and arrows.

The work of enemy Indians. Patrick ran his finger through the charcoal and red stone markings. They smeared easily. A shiver ran up his spine. *Fresh marks! I must tell Uncle Friedrich.*

Patrick turned to leave when, suddenly, he saw something move over his shoulder.

He wrapped his fingers tightly around his rifle. He shifted his eyes to the left. Then to his right. He stared ahead at the road, hoping to signal Uncle Friedrich, but the grazing horses blocked his line of sight.

If an enemy scout were to grab me, no one would notice.

Patrick felt his mouth dry up like cotton. A flood of fear washed over him as Fritz's words came echoing back: *"The poor soul who wanders from camp or lags behind—he's fair game to their savage ways."*

SEVEN

PATRICK FELT THE SKIN ON THE BACK OF his neck prickle. Someone was near. He could sense it, like an animal on the scent of its prey, only he was the prey.

With his back against the tree, he inched his rifle up along his body. He kept lifting until his hand curled around the trigger. His fingers trembled as they slipped into position. Carefully, he pulled back the flintlock with his thumb. *Click!*

Then he remembered: he hadn't taken the time to load his rifle!

As he reached into his cartridge box, he felt a hand grip his ankle.

He jumped. His gun fell to the ground with a thud. Gasping, he began twisting frantically like a rabbit caught in a snare. His leg would not come free. Even if it had, Patrick knew he could be shot in the back if he tried to escape.

He stopped struggling and glared down in horror.

There, staring up at him from the tall grass, was the darkened face of an Indian. At first, Patrick was too terrified to recognize him. But then, as his eyes caught sight of the shiny object dangling from the Indian's neck, he knew who it was.

"Gwayo!" cried Patrick, dropping down in the grass. "What are you doing here?"

"My people came to your camp last night," whispered Gwayo. "I was there, too. I saw you, but it was too late. We were sent away."

"Yes," said Patrick, "I know."

"We headed west along the river," continued Gwayo. "That's when I saw many fresh tracks in the mud—*human tracks!* The enemy . . . they come your way!"

Patrick pivoted around, searching the trees around him.

"I asked our tribe to come back," said Gwayo, "to warn your people. But our chief say, 'Let the white man fight his own battle.'"

"But you came back. Why? You could have been killed!"

"Your father. Calling out as death fell down on him—his signal kept us safe. When your father saved me, I gave my word that I will repay. When I saw the tracks, I knew what I must do. I keep my word."

Crouching low in the grass, Patrick heard a sound. He turned his head. Standing 15 paces away was a white man pointing a rifle directly at them.

"Fritz!" cried Patrick.

"Get back, Patrick!" called Fritz. "Get back, now!"

Patrick sprang to his feet. Fritz brought his rifle up to his eye. With one eye closed, he stared down the barrel of his gun. He was aiming at Gwayo.

Click!

Patrick thrust his hands out. "No—"

The explosion filled the air like a hundred-year-old tree being struck by a bolt of lightening. Gwayo fell forward into the tall grass. He didn't move.

"Is he dead?" called Fritz.

Patrick dropped down by his friend's side. A thin red stream ran out from under Gwayo's body. It was coming from his leg.

Slowly, Gwayo began to grope for his leg. Before Fritz could notice, Patrick gripped Gwayo's arm so he couldn't move.

"Y-y-yes," Patrick called out. "He's dead, sir."

Patrick could see Uncle Friedrich running up behind Fritz who was reloading his gun. "Patrick!" called Uncle Friedrich. He stopped next to Fritz. He stared ahead, worry on his face. "Patrick, are you all right?"

"Yes," said Patrick, "everything's fine." But Uncle Friedrich looked unconvinced. He moved his head this way and that, as if he were straining to see over the grass.

Fritz finished loading another shot. "Savages," he said with disgust. "One can't be too sure . . ." With his gun barrel pointed forward, Fritz began walking toward them. When he was but a few feet away, he stopped. He turned his head toward the road. Uncle Friedrich did, too.

That's when Patrick heard it: the distant crack of gunfire.

"The advance guard must be in trouble," said Fritz. He turned and began running back to the road.

"They're calling us back," said Uncle Friedrich. "Grab your gun, Patrick, and help me hitch the horses. Hurry!" Uncle Friedrich turned to leave. In the distance, Patrick could hear the wagon master calling out orders.

Patrick crouched close to his friend's ear. "I don't have much time," he whispered. He rolled Gwayo onto his back. The grass where his body lay was matted down and smeared with blood.

Patrick could see the wound just above Gwayo's knee. "Give me your knife," he said. With one quick motion, Patrick sliced through the leather thong that held the whistle. Taking the leather strip, he tied it like a tourniquet just above the wound.

"Patrick!" called Uncle Friedrich. There were more gunshots now, snapping away in the distance like pebbles hitting glass.

"You must go," said Gwayo, weakly.

"I can't leave you here," said Patrick. "They'll surely find you."

Patrick knelt behind Gwayo's head and grabbed him under his arms. He tried to drag him behind a large rock, but Gwayo was too heavy. "Stay low," Patrick told him. "I *will* be back for you. I promise!"

Coming out through the trees, Patrick heard the roll of a volley followed by the crash of heavy fire. *Enemy fire*, thought Patrick. *Gwayo was right. The enemy must have been waiting for us.*

Quickly, he recovered his gun next to the tree.

"Hurry, Patrick!" called Uncle Friedrich.

Patrick grabbed the harness of the last remaining horse and hitched it to the wagon.

"The enemy is attacking the advance guard," said Uncle Friedrich. "They came upon them about a half mile from here. We must come to their aid."

As Patrick prepared to jump into the wagon, Uncle Friedrich said, "Load your gun, Patrick. Be ready."

Dirt flew up from the road as the wagon surged forward, enveloping them in a cloud of brown and gray. Other wagons followed behind, rushing headlong to the sound of the firing.

Patrick laid the gun across his lap and rested the barrel in the crook of his left arm. Quickly, he opened his cartridge pouch and pulled out a brown paper tube. Inside the paper tube was some gunpowder and a lead musket ball. He bit off the twisted paper end and poured the gunpowder down the barrel. Then he crumpled the brown paper and stuffed it with the musket ball into the mouth of the barrel.

Taking the ramrod, he slid it down the muzzle, packing the ball and powder tightly, the way his father had shown him so many times before. Satisfied that the ball was in its proper place, he replaced the ramrod under the gun barrel.

Finally, he tapped a measure of grains from his powder horn into the priming pan. Replacing the cap on his powder horn, he reviewed the steps in his mind, careful not to have missed one.

Patrick's stomach tightened as he pictured what

he might find when they reached the front line. He wondered if he'd be able to pull the trigger if he saw the enemy—the men Mr. MacDermott said were responsible for his father's death.

As the wagon pressed forward, the sound of the firing grew louder and sharper. Patrick concentrated on holding his gun with the muzzle pointing up, so as not to lose the ball and powder.

As they came around a bend in the road, Patrick heard a terrible, horrible sound that made his skin turn clammy: the war cry of Indians.

EIGHT

A TERRIFIC BURST OF INDIAN WAR whoops rose from the front. The shouts and screeches sounded more like those of animals than humans. Never before had Patrick heard such a horrifying sound. *Why*, Patrick wondered, *isn't the advance guard silencing them?*

Peering out of the wagon, Patrick watched as row upon row of British regulars marched in precision toward the sound. They looked so powerful in their crimson uniforms and high caps. But as Patrick looked at their faces, he saw one thing more uniform than their identical outfits: fear.

The wagon came to a sudden stop. The soldiers did, too. Patrick jumped out and looked up the road. Racing toward them was the advance guard. They were running up the road like sheep pursued by wolves. "The Indians are upon us!" cried one.

"HALT! HALT!" screamed a corporal. The men ignored the command and kept running toward Patrick's division.

Why are they running toward us? wondered

Patrick. *They're supposed to be advancing. These men are retreating!*

At once Patrick found himself in the middle of a mass of frightened men. They were huddled all around him, British regulars and colonial troops alike, seemingly unable or unwilling to follow the officers' orders.

"In line, men! *IN LINE!*"

Patrick could see nothing but the backs of the men around him. The soldiers, their once-fine military lines now broken, were bunched together, facing out toward the enemy in no particular formation. Patrick struggled to hold his gun upright as warm bodies began pressing in around him.

He whipped his head around, frantically searching for any sign of Uncle Friedrich or the wagon. But as gunshots and Indian war cries sounded all about him, Patrick found himself being swept farther away by the crowd. As they huddled in the middle of the twelve-foot road the army had cleared, Patrick tried to see past the soldiers. He couldn't see the wagons or a single Frenchman or Indian. *Where are they?*

A man standing next to Patrick fired his gun. For several seconds, Patrick could hear nothing but a high-pitched ring. Smoke stung his eyes. The air stank of gun oil and acrid smoke. His head started pounding. Everyone around him was either firing or reloading his rifle.

"I can't see a single Frenchman!" cried a British regular behind Patrick.

"The French have brought their Indians, hordes

of them!" cried someone. "And if there are any French soldiers, they're probably stripped to the waist like Indians. They're all hiding behind trees and rocks!"

"Savage cowards!" cried another.

Standing there, Patrick could hear the eerie screams of the Indians, but he, too, couldn't see them. It was as though he had entered a den of invisible lions. *Where are you, Uncle Friedrich? Where are you?*

Behind Patrick came a loud thud. He turned to see a British regular lying on the ground, his vest drenched in blood.

Patrick felt his knees grow weak. His stomach began to churn and swirl as if he had eaten something rotten. He cupped his hand to his mouth to keep from getting sick.

"They've taken the hill!" cried a man next to Patrick. He pointed to a hillock on their right, north of the road. At its peak it measured the height of about four covered wagons stacked one on top of the other. "They're firing on us from up on that hill!"

Patrick could see puffs of gun smoke rise from several points along the hill's ridge.

Thud! Another man fell. Then another. Men were falling to the ground like dead leaves in autumn. Some cried out for help, others cursed their invisible foe. Some couldn't make a sound at all.

"They're coming at us from both sides!" called someone. "It's a three-sided trap!"

I simply must get to Uncle Friedrich! Turning, Patrick forced his way through the crowd. With his gun gripped tightly in his hands, he stumbled forward, ducking past men with their guns pointing out in every direction.

"Charge the hill, men!" cried a colonial officer on horseback. "Char—" The officer stopped, sucked in his breath, and clutched his right side. His horse reared up, flung the officer to the ground, and raced off toward the woods.

Suddenly Patrick saw a tall figure on horseback appear to his left. *Could it be?* He rode up alongside General Braddock. As the tall man called out to the General, Patrick could see that it was George Washington.

"General," said Washington, "permission sought, sir, to send a troop to charge the northern hill in the Indian manner."

General Braddock shook his head. "No. Direct these men to form their lines!"

Through the drifting haze of gun smoke, Patrick could see to the right at the base of the hill a mounted officer in a blue militia coat. Too far away to hear the General's orders, the officer began leading a group of provincials to the trunk of a great fallen tree at the base of the hill. From there, he ordered his men to charge the hill's steep bank.

"Frenchmen!" cried a British regular next to Patrick. He leveled his gun and fired at the provincials sloping the hill.

"No!" cried Patrick. Smoke engulfed him. He coughed, gasping for air. When the smoke lifted, Patrick saw others around him firing at the backs of the men scaling the ridge. "Those are our men!" cried Patrick. "You're shooting at your own troops!" But the roar of muskets drowned out his cries.

"Hold your fire, men!" said a voice. Patrick could see Washington riding up near the base of the hill. With his sword held high overhead, Washington positioned himself squarely between the confused mass of soldiers firing away and the provincials charging up the hill. "Hold your fire, men!" commanded Washington. *"HOLD FIRE!"*

While bullets rained down from the Indians atop the hill, Washington, his back to the Indians, acted as a cover for the surviving provincials as they retreated safely from the hill.

The air reeked of spent powder and sweat. Patrick spun around, searching for the wagon train. *There it was!* With all his strength, he pushed his way past the men, stumbling over dead and dying bodies. The army's twelve-foot wide road now looked like one giant open grave.

When he finally reached the wagon, Uncle Friedrich was nowhere in sight. "Uncle Friedrich?" he called.

"He's gone," said a voice.

Turning around, Patrick recognized the man as one of the wagoners who had followed them that morning.

"He went looking for yeh," continued the man. "He wants yeh to take the wagon back with the rear guard and stay put. He's sick with worry about yeh."

Patrick stood transfixed, unsure of what he should

do. *I can't leave Uncle Friedrich,* he told himself. *How will he ever find me?* Ignoring the man's instructions, Patrick climbed up and stood on one of the wagon wheels. He scanned the crowd of soldiers, searching for Uncle Friedrich's weathered brown hat. There were too many to count.

"Didn't you hear me, boy?" scolded the man.

Patrick wanted to tell him that the plan was all wrong. But the man shook his head at Patrick as if he were a child. "Go on. Git!"

Patrick swung up on the wheel horse. He held his gun across his lap with his left hand, taking hold of the reins with his right. He gave the reins a snap. The horses didn't move. Then Patrick remembered his uncle's command for turning left. In a deep, loud voice he called out, "Yee! Yee!"

The team stepped out, turning left as commanded.

As Patrick turned to face the road, he froze. "Whoa! Whoa!" he shouted.

Thundering toward him at full speed was part of the rear guard. Mounted officers with swords drawn shouted commands, ordering their men forward to reinforce the men under fire. The advancing soldiers and their supply wagons choked the passageway to the river, leaving no room for Patrick's wagon to pass.

Patrick glanced back over his shoulder at the mass of troops huddled there. *I'm trapped!*

NINE

UNABLE TO MOVE THE WAGON MORE than a few feet from the spot where Uncle Friedrich had left it, Patrick jumped off his mount and into the sea of armed men. As he picked his way through the crowd, scanning the faces for Uncle Friedrich, musket balls screamed past his ears. Riderless horses galloped frantically in every direction, crazy with terror. The crowd seemed to be bunching in tighter and tighter, squeezing Patrick until he thought he'd be trampled underfoot.

"Make way!" cried someone behind Patrick.

Two British soldiers were dragging a wooden cart through the crowd. Escorting them on horseback was George Washington. *Perhaps he has seen Uncle Friedrich!*

As Patrick pushed his way toward Washington, he could see the uniformed legs of a British officer poking out from the moving cart. Who it was, Patrick couldn't tell.

"Colonel Washington!" called Patrick. Just then,

someone grabbed Patrick's shirt from behind and flung him backwards onto the ground.

"Out of the way, boy!" screamed a British regular. "Can't you see General Braddock is injured? If they don't get him off the field, the enemy will have their way with him!"

By the time Patrick scrambled to his feet, Washington was too deep into the crowd for Patrick to reach him.

My rifle! Patrick snatched it up from the ground. He checked it carefully; he wanted to make sure the lead ball hadn't come loose from the muzzle when he fell to the ground.

"The General's dead!" cried a man in the crowd.

"We don't know that!" cried another.

"They've taken down almost every mounted officer and now the General!" said the man next to Patrick. "We're nothin' but target practice!"

"I'm not leaving 'til I get orders!" called someone behind him.

The man beside Patrick lowered his gun and looked about. He licked his lips like a nervous dog. "I've a family to think about," he said in a low tone. Turning, he ducked through the crowd and headed back toward the river. Others followed.

"They'll hang you for desertion!" warned another as they passed.

The crowd opened enough for Patrick to move deeper into the mass. As he squeezed past a soldier reloading his rifle, he stumbled upon a man sitting up on the ground. His brown hat bore a familiar

crease just above the man's left ear.

"Uncle Friedrich!" Stooping down, Patrick saw a gaping wound in his uncle's right hand.

"Patrick, you're here!" said Uncle Friedrich. "God bless you, lad. Here. Help me wrap my hand."

Patrick took the strip of cloth from his uncle and finished tying off the bandage. "We've got to get back to the wagon," said Patrick. He grabbed his uncle under his arms and helped him to his feet.

When they reached the spot where the train of wagons stood, Patrick's mouth dropped. Surrounding their Conestoga wagon were dozens of abandoned wagon beds. The horses had been cut free. The leather leads hung uselessly in the dust.

"The wagoners must have retreated across the river," said Uncle Friedrich.

"What do we do now?" asked Patrick.

"The road is too crowded for our wagon to pass," said Uncle Friedrich. "We'll have to cut our own horses loose and leave the wagon bed behind."

Patrick thought of Aunt Netta. She had been so worried about losing their horses and wagon. He looked at Uncle Friedrich. His face was pale and sallow. Blood had already soaked through his bandage. *The most important thing is to get Uncle Friedrich home to Aunt Netta.*

Patrick cut the horses loose. He tied all but one of them together with a rope, just as he used to do when he and his father fastened the packhorses together before a trip to the trading post. He helped Uncle Friedrich up on the wheel horse and placed the reins in his good hand.

"Well, let's go, Patrick," said Uncle Friedrich. "Get your horse."

"I—I can't. Not yet," said Patrick. "There's something I must do first. I'll meet you where we camped last night, just beyond the second crossing of the Monongahela."

"No!" said his uncle sharply. "I won't permit it! It's much too dangerous!"

"I'm sorry, Uncle Friedrich. But I gave my word."

"Patrick!"

"I'll explain later." Patrick gave Uncle Friedrich's horse a slap on his hind; the horse trotted off down the road, pulling the two horses behind it.

As Patrick turned to mount his horse, a voice raged above the din: "Take the high ground, men! General's orders!" It was George Washington, riding with his sword held high in the air. "Charge the hill!" he called again.

As Patrick looked on, Washington's horse suddenly collapsed to the ground.

"Colonel Washington!" Patrick began running towards him. He could see the great man scrambling to get up on his hands and knees. In an instant, Washington had sprung to his feet.

Patrick spotted Washington's tricornered hat just a few feet away. He picked it up. Dusting the dirt from its brim, Patrick saw a hole in the top where a musket ball had entered. Looking at Washington, Patrick could see that the bullet had missed him.

"Your hat, sir," said Patrick.

Washington turned toward him. Patrick could see that his face was still pale from sickness. *How, Patrick wondered, can a man so ill lead men in battle so gallantly?*

"Patrick, why are you still here?" asked Washington. "You must go back with the other wagoners, across the river where it's safe." He took the hat and placed it on his head. As he did, Patrick glanced down at Washington's uniform. He counted four slits in his vest. *Bullets holes, but no blood! Not a single bullet or tomahawk has pierced his flesh!*

Washington shook his head. "We shall never gain the day unless we take the rising ground!" Washington suddenly lunged out, grabbing the reins of a riderless horse trotting past. In an instant, he was back in the saddle, pointing his sword to the hill north of the road. "Take the hill!" he called again.

Patrick mounted his horse. As he maneuvered through the tangle of abandoned wagon beds, he saw a young man crouching down with his back against a wagon wheel. His stringy blond hair dangled in his face as he fumbled with the lock on his rifle. Just then, Patrick noticed an Indian creeping up behind the wagon. His face was smeared with paint, red and black. His eyes remained fixed on his intended victim as he crept ever closer.

Looking back at the young man with the rifle, Patrick saw who the intended victim was.

"Will!"

TEN

"**B**EHIND YOU, WILL!" SCREAMED Patrick.

Will whipped his head around, peering beneath the wagon through the spokes of the giant wheel.

The Indian was closing in quickly. Patrick could see there was no way Will could ready his gun in time. In one swift motion, Patrick swung his rifle into position and leveled it at the Indian.

He fired.

There was a blinding flash, a roar, and a great explosion with such force that it thrust Patrick backward, almost pulling him off his horse.

When the smoke lifted, Patrick saw the Indian sprawled out on the ground, motionless. At first, he wasn't sure he was the one who had killed him. Then, finding no marksman within range, he knew his answer. Part of him felt sickened for having taken a man's life. Then he recalled the wagon master's words: "After all, this *is* war."

I had to do it. Papa would have said so if he were here.

Will didn't say anything. Instead, he stared back at Patrick through dazed eyes, his face as dingy gray as his filthy shirt.

Patrick took off down the road, urging his horse faster and faster. As the rattle of muskets droned on behind him, Patrick wondered if he would find Gwayo alive. He wondered, too, if by now the enemy had begun to circle around toward the rear in an attempt to close off any escape route and attack the baggage train. *Either way, I have to try. I gave Gwayo my word.*

Glancing over his shoulder, Patrick could see more soldiers retreating. The troops, pale from fear, hunger, and weariness, appeared more as spirits than men. They were running towards him, scrambling up the same road they had marched down so calmly only two hours before. Patrick wondered. *Is the enemy on their heels, coming this way?*

As Patrick came to a familiar copse of trees, he slowed his horse. His eyes scanned the tree line for the familiar oak where the bark had been stripped away. As he did, he kept his hands firmly on his rifle. *I should reload,* he told himself. *No—I haven't time.* He could hear the pounding footsteps of the men running up the road behind him. *I must find Gwayo!*

Spotting the oak, Patrick swung off his horse and led him into the woods. Quickly he found the large rock where he had tried to pull his friend to safety.

"Gwayo!" he called out softly.

Slowly, a face appeared next to the rock. "Patrick?"

Dropping to his knees, Patrick examined Gwayo's

leg. It was covered in blood. "We've got to go before any unfriendlies find us," he told him. He turned around, facing the road. "We can't take the road. The regulars may mistake you for the enemy. We'll have to make our way through the woods, staying east of the river." He looked at Gwayo and smiled. "We'll discover a new footpath. Just like old times."

Patrick helped Gwayo to a standing position. Placing his shoulder against his horse, Patrick laced his fingers together. "Here," he said, resting his clasped hands against his thigh. "Step up with your good leg. Careful, now."

Wincing, Gwayo did as Patrick instructed. But when his body had made it halfway up, he stopped. His wounded leg dangled uselessly against his body as if it were a foreign object.

"Use your arms!" cried Patrick. "You can do it!" Patrick pushed from behind with all his might. Gwayo grabbed hold of the horse's mane and pulled. Finally, he was up.

Taking the reins, Patrick led them away from the road of retreating soldiers and deeper into the woods. He wanted to take the horse to a trot, but he knew Gwayo's leg couldn't stand such jostling. He walked in silence, keeping watch for a stray Indian or soldier.

They crossed Turtle Creek and made their way through the Narrows along the east bank of the Monongahela. They kept on, carefully picking their way through the heavily wooded forest, choked with bushes and clumps of rank ferns.

*   *   *

Darkness was falling when they reached the point where the retreating soldiers would have crossed the Monongahela a second time. Patrick found the road the army had blazed earlier that morning and followed it up over the rise and toward the clearing where they had all camped the night before. Somewhere deep in the woods he could hear the cries of wounded men who had collapsed during their retreat, unable to go any farther. Patrick knew he couldn't help them, but their cries haunted him as he plodded on toward the campsite. With every step, Patrick felt the muscles in his legs and feet throb as if he, too, might collapse. He pushed on, too hungry and too tired to say a word.

As they entered the clearing of the campsite where Uncle Friedrich was to meet him, Patrick stopped. He looked around. All he could find was a torn up boot, a pile of cold ashes, and scraps of cartridge paper lying about.

Patrick dropped his chin to his chest and closed his eyes. In that dark moment, he pictured what might have happened to his uncle. He thought of Aunt Netta and the children and how much they depended on Uncle Friedrich. *I should never have left him! Never!*

Then from across the clearing came a strong voice calling out, "Patrick!"

Turning, Patrick looked to the far edge of the field where a neat row of pine trees stood. There was

Uncle Friedrich sitting atop his wheel horse. He still had the two horses attached by the rope, just as Patrick had left them.

Patrick took off in a run toward his uncle. His legs moved with remarkable quickness that belied the exhaustion that weighed so heavily just moments before.

They met in the middle of the clearing. Uncle Friedrich swung down off his horse and, with his bandaged hand, wrapped both arms around Patrick, pulling him in tight.

"Thank God you're alive!" said Uncle Friedrich. "Washington came through here not long ago. Said the General had been fatally shot. He was forced to order a retreat to spare the remaining men. So when I didn't see you with him . . ."

"Colonel Washington is alive? The enemy was firing at him, Uncle Friedrich. I saw where his uniform had been ripped by bullets!"

Uncle Friedrich smiled. "George Washington is destined to fight another day."

"Yes," said Patrick thoughtfully. "Perhaps he is being protected for some important duty in the future."

"You may be right, Patrick." Uncle Friedrich looked beyond to where Gwayo sat upon the horse. His smile suddenly vanished. "Who is he?"

"A good friend. Come, I want you to meet him."

Patrick introduced Uncle Friedrich to Gwayo. "Gwayo was with me the night Papa was killed. And he was here, today, to warn me of enemy tracks he had found along the river."

"It is Patrick who deserves praise," said Gwayo. "He saved my life. He came back for me just as he said he would. He is a man of courage and honor, just like his father."

Hearing this, Patrick said nothing. Instead, he let the words sink into his head, his heart. And then, in that instant, Patrick recalled his father's words: *Courage is doing what you have to do even when you're scared.*

Patrick looked at Gwayo. *'Twas easy to save Gwayo's life*, he thought. *I did it without thinking because he is a friend, a loyal friend. But what about Will?* He thought of how Will had treated him over the past several weeks, so different from Gwayo. *Was Will equally deserving of being saved?*

Yes, thought Patrick finally. *Will was simply a comrade, a fellow soldier fighting against a common foe.* And yet Patrick was certain that Will, having been humbled in battle, would return home a better man than when he left.

"I must get back to my people," said Gwayo.

"But your leg—you'll never make it alone," said Patrick. He turned to Uncle Friedrich. "Mingo Town is too far to walk. We'll have to take him on our horse."

Uncle Friedrich shook his head. "We'll be killed if we do. That's French territory."

Patrick was silent. Then, turning to Gwayo he said, "Come with us. We'll meet up with Colonel Washington and the rest of the troops at Colonel

Dunbar's camp. I know the surgeon. He'll mend your leg as good as new and then you can return home."

Gwayo hesitated.

"Don't worry," said Patrick. "Colonel Washington will see to it that no one harms you. You'll be safe with us."

Gwayo finally agreed.

As the three of them turned to leave, Patrick felt a sense of peace overcome him. His father had been right: everything was going to be all right. After all, his father would say, he still had his gun and his horse.

Historical Postscript

Anyone studying the Battle of the Monongahela[1] may wonder how a well-trained British fighting force of roughly 1,500 soldiers could be defeated by a French and Indian force approximating 850.[2] To discover the answer, one must consider the facts leading up to the fateful day of July 9, 1755.

In the early part of the eighteenth century, the land west of the Appalachian Mountains was principally occupied by Native Americans. Trappers and frontiersmen—both French and English—soon saw that the land was rich with resources and provided new opportunities for settlement. In order to claim the region for themselves, both France and England began building forts to stake claim to the territory. This set the stage for what would later become known as the French and Indian War (1754-1763).

One of the most desirable sites for a fort was an area in western Pennsylvania called the Forks of the Ohio, where the Allegheny and Monongahela Rivers joined to form the Ohio River (present-day

---

[1] Other names for the Battle of the Monongahela include "Braddock's Defeat" and the "Battle of the Wilderness."
[2] The exact number of French and Indians is unknown.

Pittsburgh). In early 1754, a British fort, Fort Prince George, was constructed there on orders of Virginia Governor Robert Dinwiddie. George Washington himself had recommended to Dinwiddie the location of the new fort. To ensure easy access to Fort Prince George, Dinwiddie ordered Washington, a lieutenant colonel of the Virginia Militia, to lead a contingent of Virginia troops to clear a road to the Forks and reinforce the men stationed there. In April, 1754, however, before Washington and his troops could reach the fort, the French attacked and captured it. They immediately began constructing a new French fort, to be called Fort Duquesne (due-CANE).

Washington and his troops, having learned that the fort was in French hands, discovered and attacked a French scouting party on May 28, 1754. They killed 10 Frenchmen and captured 22 prisoners in what became known as the "Jumonville Affair." A month later, the French retaliated by attacking Washington and his troops, forcing him to surrender at Fort Necessity in the "Great Meadows" of southwestern Pennsylvania. Now firmly established, Fort Duquesne gave the French command of the Ohio Valley.

The British, however, did not give up. Early the following year, 1755, the British sent General Edward Braddock to the colonies as commander-in-chief of the British forces in America. One of his goals was to capture Fort Duquesne and thus take control of the region. Upon hearing favorable reports about Washington, General Braddock personally invited the twenty-three-year-old to join his military family as one of his assistants, or "aides-de-camp." Although this was a volunteer position without pay, Washington eagerly accepted. He wanted to prove himself to General Braddock and ultimately earn a permanent position in the British army.

On May 30, 1755, the British army set out from its base at Fort Cumberland (present-day Cumberland, Maryland) and began the arduous 112-mile march northwest to Fort Duquesne. The force included two British regiments, colonial militiamen, and volunteer colonial men and women. Postmaster General Dr. Benjamin Franklin was instrumental in procuring the necessary wagons, drivers, and horses for the campaign. One such colonial wagon driver was a frontiersman named Daniel Boone. He is believed to have helped transport the army's supplies.

Before the army could proceed to the Forks, however, a road twelve feet wide had to be blazed through the wilderness to accommodate the army's 2,000 soldiers (approximately 1,500 fighting men and 500 support people), 200 wagons, various artillery pieces, and supplies. The army marched European-style in long rows of men, three- or four-abreast. Progress was slow, averaging only three miles a day. Bridges had to be erected over creeks and high spots had to be leveled to accommodate the wagons. Still, wagons frequently broke down or became stuck in the steep and rocky terrain. Horses, too, grew weary under the weight of their packs. To speed their travel, Braddock acted on Washington's advice and divided the army into two groups. A lighter, quicker force advanced ahead, while the majority of the wagons and supplies followed behind at a slower pace.

Other problems arose as well. Washington became ill with a life-threatening fever that lasted for days. Despite his protests, Washington was ordered by General Braddock to drop back until he was healthy enough to rejoin the march. That day would not come until July 8, one day before the Battle of the Monongahela would begin.

Indians, both those friendly to the British and those allied with the French, proved to be an important factor in the campaign. On more than one occasion, certain groups of Indians, principally members of the Six Nations Confederacy (known to the French as the Iroquois), offered to help the British fight against the French. Waging war in the dense forests of America presented different obstacles than those found in the open battlefields of Europe. Washington advocated to Braddock using the Indians as scouts, as well as employing their style of wilderness fighting, which was suited to the terrain. These tactics included ambushes, fighting from behind rocks and trees, and zigzagging toward the enemy. General Braddock, however, was not convinced. His extensive military experience was in the European manner of warfare, characterized by tightly packed rows of soldiers standing in straight lines, facing the enemy, and firing on command. He didn't understand the practicality of ambush and withdrawal, a tactic that saved Indian lives while maximizing military impact. Rather, Braddock believed the Indians' style of guerilla warfare was cowardly and undisciplined. His views offended the Indians, turning many away. At times Braddock openly refused their help altogether. Spurning Indian aid would come to be regarded as a fateful mistake, as Braddock himself would later confess on his deathbed.

By 2:00 p.m. on July 9, Braddock and Washington had led the army across the second ford of the Monongahela River. Only seven miles from Fort Duquesne, the British army spotted a man dressed as an enemy Indian running toward them. The "Indian" was French captain Daniel de Beaujeu, and he was not alone. Hiding in a nearby ravine was a force of roughly 70 French regulars, 140 Canadian militiamen, and 640 Indians.[3] Beaujeu had originally planned to have his men lay in wait on the banks of the Monongahela and attack the British as they crossed the river. However, when Beaujeu discovered that the British had already crossed the river, the French captain quickly ordered his men to hide in the ravine until he gave his signal. Upon Beaujeu's command, his men sprang forth with loud shrieks and muskets firing. The sudden attack caught the British advance guard by surprise. Although greatly outnumbered, the French force used the Indian style of warfare and the natural elements to their advantage, taking aim from behind rocks and trees. The

[3] See Footnote 2.

British soldiers, unable to see their intended targets through the dense terrain, fired wildly into the woods. The frightening Indian war cries and continuous rain of musket balls streaming in from an invisible enemy caused the British army to panic. Despite officers' orders to form their military lines and attack as they had been trained, the British force instead huddled together in the middle of the road they had cleared only moments earlier. There they were an easy target for their enemy. One by one the bodies fell. From their huddled mass, the frightened British and colonial soldiers leveled and fired their muskets in desperation, at times mistakenly shooting their own comrades in the back.

The Battle of the Monongahela lasted for more than two hours. It was a rout. Of the British force's 1,459 fighting men, 977 were killed, wounded, or lost. General Braddock was wounded during the battle as well, and died four days later. George Washington, however, miraculously survived. At over six feet tall, Washington knew he presented an easy target on horseback. Writing to his brother John after the battle, Washington wrote:

". . . by the all-powerful dispensations of Providence, I have been protected beyond all human probability or expectation; for I had four bullets through my coat, and two horses shot under me, yet escaped unhurt, although death was leveling my companions on every side of me!"

Though hostilities had started nearly two years earlier, war wasn't officially declared between

France and England until 1756.[4] It wasn't until 1758 that the British finally began to take the upper hand. On November 24, 1758, as British General John Forbes led a force of 6,000 to advance on Fort Duquesne, the French quickly abandoned the fort without a fight, burning much of it before they left. The British built a new fort on the same site and named it Fort Pitt in honor of England's Prime Minister William Pitt. Fort Pitt was revered as one of Britain's largest and most elaborate fortresses in all of North America.

---

[4] France and England didn't limit their aggressions against each other to turf battles on American soil. The Seven Years' War (1756-1763), of which the French and Indian War was a part, was also fought across Europe, India, the Caribbean islands, the Philippines, and Africa. The Seven Years' War— which, of course, wasn't called that until it was over—involved not just England and France, but every major nation in Europe.